First published by Parragon in 2011

Parragon
Queen Street House
4 Queen Street
Bath BA1 1HE, UK

www.chuggington.com
© Ludorum plc 2011

ISBN 978-1-4454-3547-3

Printed in China

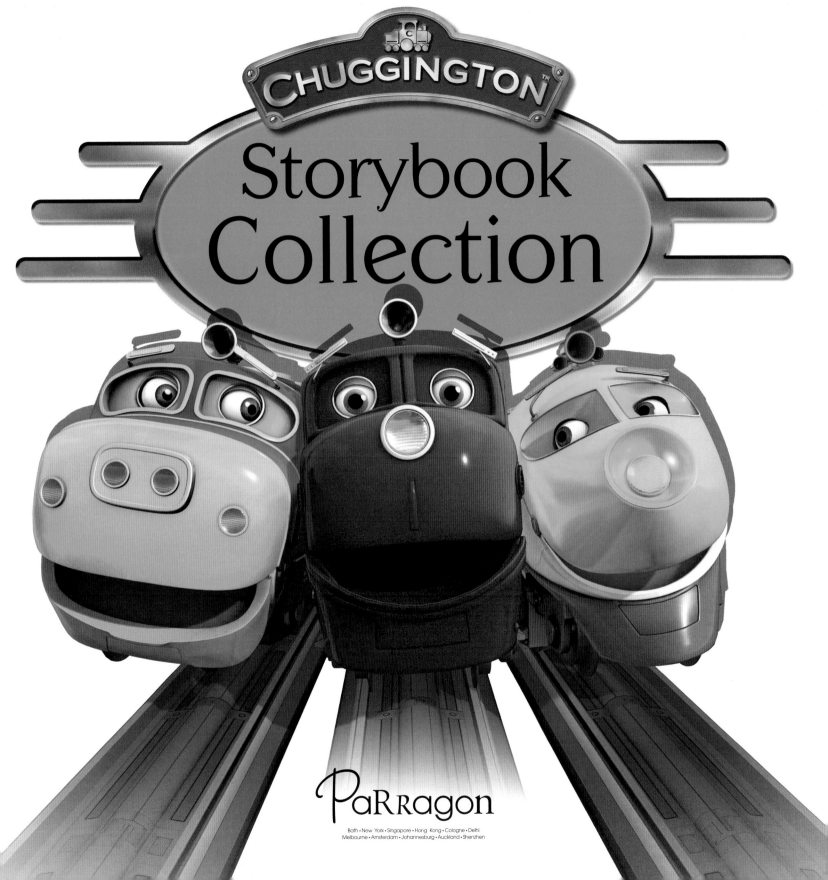

CHUGGINGTON™

Storybook Collection

PaRragon

Bath • New York • Singapore • Hong Kong • Cologne • Delhi
Melbourne • Amsterdam • Johannesburg • Auckland • Shenzhen

Contents

Wilson Gets a Wash

One day, the trainees were playing hide and seek in the park. Brewster closed his eyes while Koko and Wilson looked for places to hide.

"One, two, three..." counted Brewster, as Koko hid.

"Eighteen, nineteen, twenty," he called, as Wilson zipped around behind him.

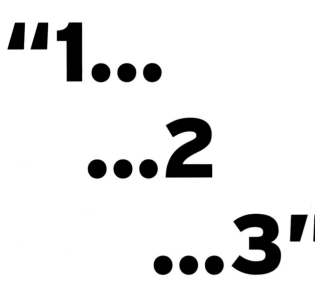

"1...

...2

...3"

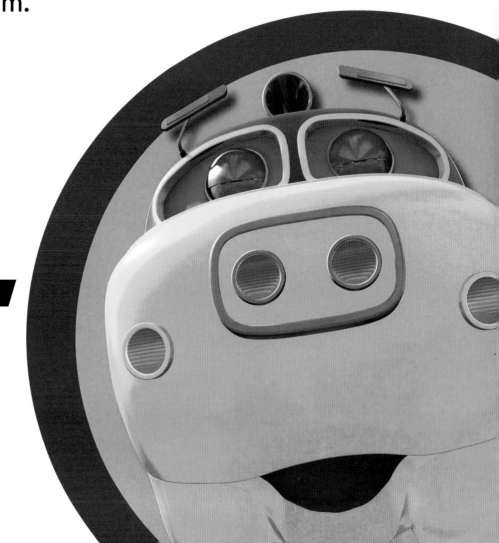

"Ready or not, here I come!" Brewster shouted. "I see you, Koko!" he chuckled.

"Ooooohh," Koko sighed, sad that he had found her so quickly.

Brewster trundled on, looking for Wilson. Where was that chugger?

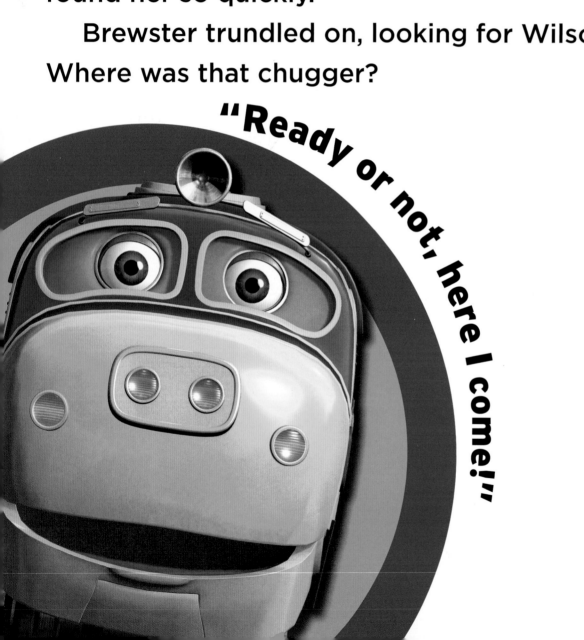

"Ready or not, here I come!"

All the while, Wilson was sneaking along behind his friend.

"I give up!" Brewster yelled.

"Wahay! Here I am!" shouted Wilson, honking his horn.

"Wow, you're the best hidey-chugger ever!" Brewster laughed as they rode to the training yard.

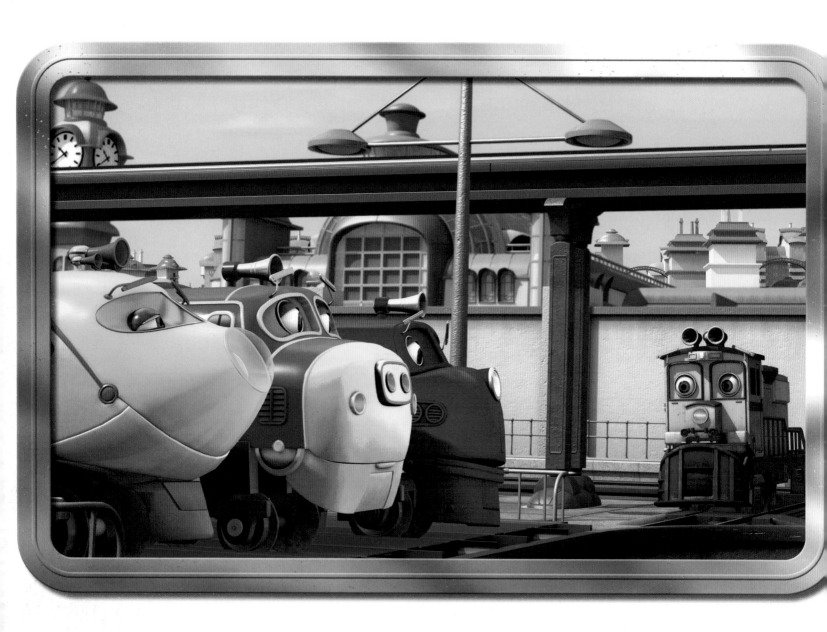

At the training yard, Dunbar was teaching the trainees how to brake in different weather conditions.

"Brilliant Brewster!" Dunbar called, when Brewster braked well on some dry leaves.

"Here I come!" cried Wilson, as he sped down the track. The leaves scattered everywhere, blowing up into his face so he couldn't see.

"Go slower!" Dunbar scolded, when Wilson skidded and banged into the bumpers.

screeeech!

Crash!

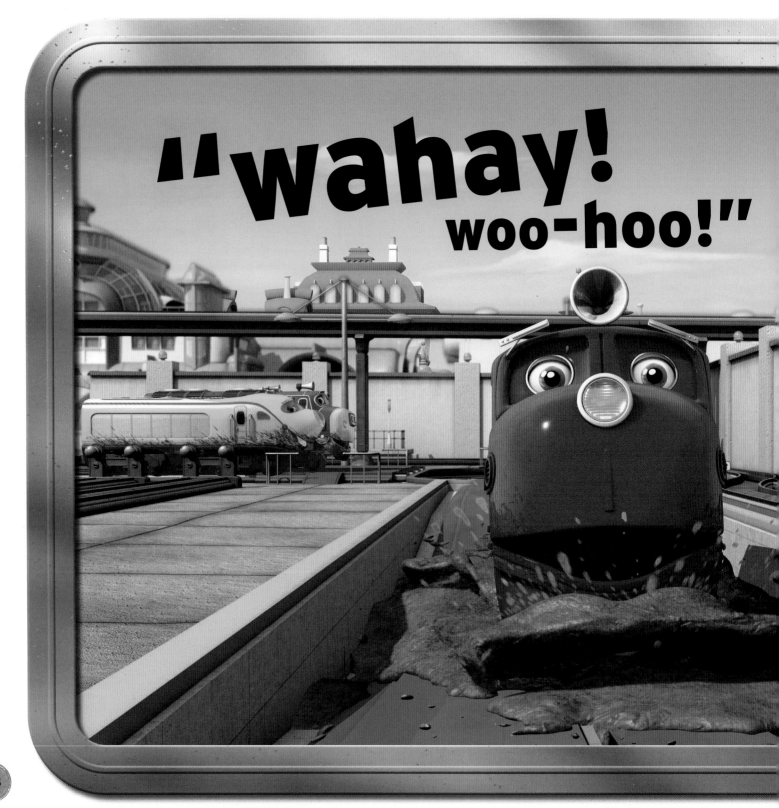

Next, Dunbar put mud on the rails. Wilson zoomed into the big puddle and splashed mud everywhere!

"Wahoo, Wahay! Woo-hoo!" he shouted as he went back and forth through the mud, getting really messy.

"All of you report to Lori for a clean up," said Dunbar.

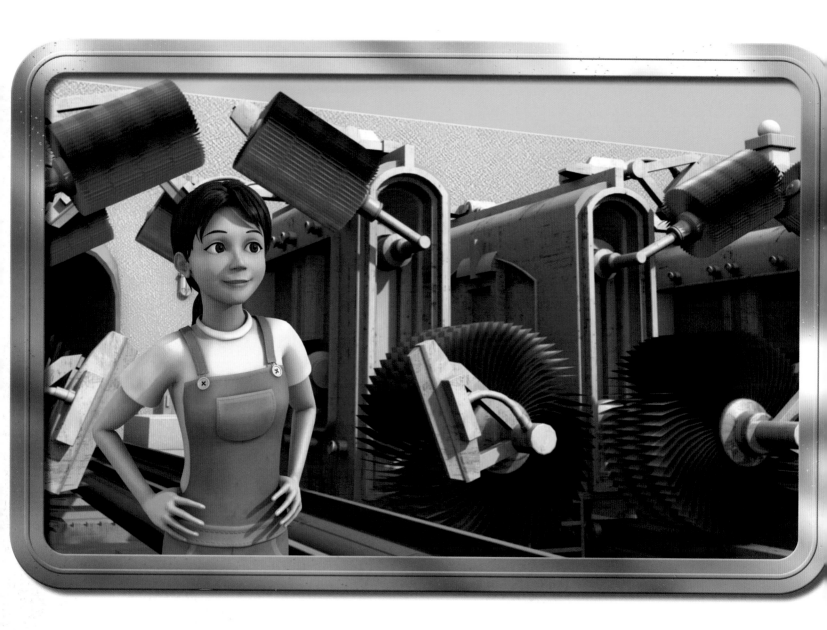

"UGH!"

When Koko, Brewster and Wilson arrived at the fuel yard, Lori showed them the new chuggwash.

"It's like a great big shower for chuggers," she said. Wilson wasn't so sure he wanted to be clean.

"Ugh," he said to Peckham the dog, "Let's sneak away!"

Wilson rolled into the recycling yard and hid from Irving, who was sorting out the rubbish.

Suddenly, Irving tipped his load of rubbish straight into Wilson's hiding place. Being dirty was so much fun, Wilson decided to go and find more mucky things.

"Wowzer!"

"Wahay!" called Wilson, as he sped into a mound of fresh grass in the park. "Messy, grassy, mess, mess, mess!" he sang.

"Whoa," he cried, slamming on the brakes just before a water sprinkler. "That was close. I nearly got clean!"

Meanwhile, at the depot, Koko and Brewster looked shiny and clean.

"Where did Wilson get to?" asked Lori.

"Don't worry, we'll find him," said Koko.

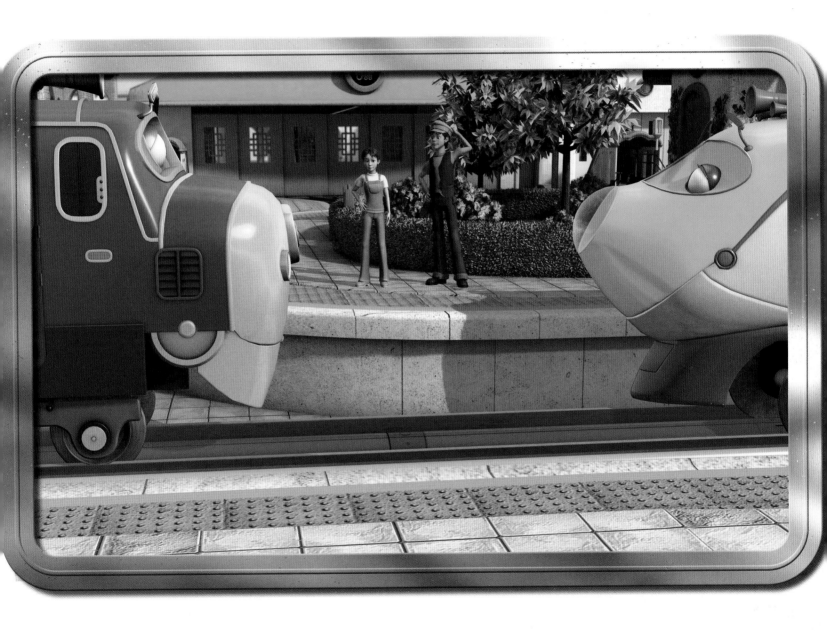

"Tee hee!"

"Tee hee!"

28

Dirty Wilson saw Koko and Brewster searching for him and quickly hid from his friends.

"Mucky is more fun," he giggled.

Koko had a good idea to trap Wilson on the rails.

"Gotcha!" Koko cried, and they towed their naughty friend to the chuggwash.

"Gotcha!"

"Noooo. Please don't make me," Wilson moaned as they got to the fuel yard.

"It's really fun, Wilson," Brewster said. Spinning brushes tickled Wilson behind the gears.

"Oooo, actually, it feels quite nice!" he giggled. "I can't wait to get dirty again, then I can come back to the chuggwash."

Koko and the Squirrels

One morning, Vee asked Koko to go to the timber yard.

"I can't wait! I'm ready for my tunnel colour, Vee," Koko said excitedly.

"Aren't you forgetting something Koko?" Vee said.

Just then, Old Puffer Pete rolled up to the platform, ready to get his tunnel colour too.

Puff
Puff
Puff

"Watch the board for your tunnel colour," Vee said as the colours started to flash.

"But I was here first," grumbled Koko.

"When I was your age, this was all done with coloured flags," Pete said. Koko rolled her eyes. She had heard that story before.

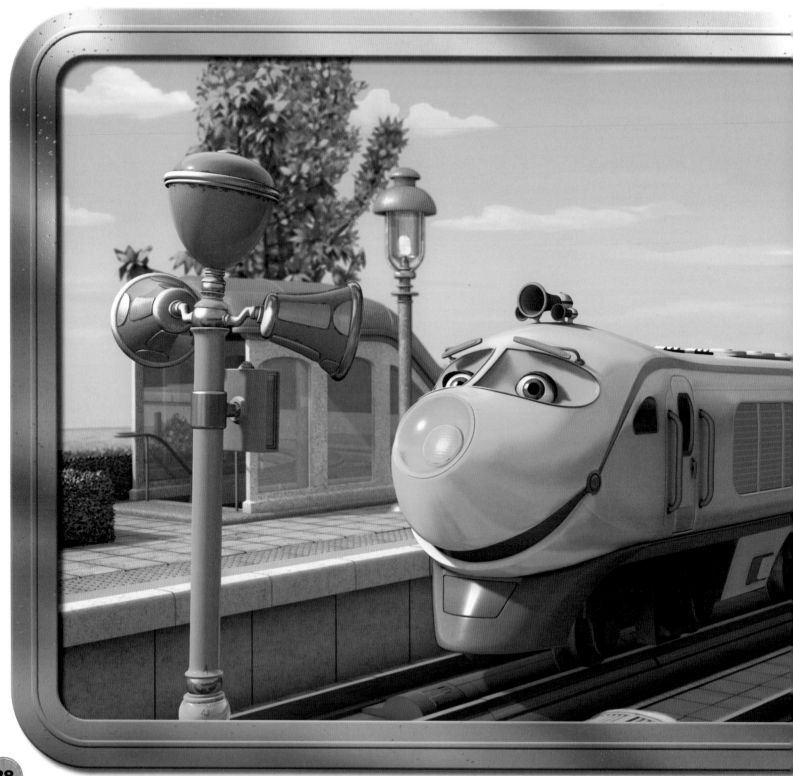

"Is it my turn now?" Koko asked with relief when Pete had gone towards the green tunnel. But Koko had forgotten a flatcar to carry the timber!

"Back in two clackety-clacks," she called.

Clackety clack!

At the rolling stock yard, Dunbar tried to help Koko buckle up to a flatcar.

"Back up sloooowly," he said, but Koko was too excited about her day to stay still. It was boring to go slow.

"I'm going to chugga chugg all the way to the timber yard and then chugga chugg to the paper mill," she said.

Meanwhile, Old Puffer Pete was enjoying his trip, when two squirrels jumped onto his roof.

"Oh! Hello Mr. Squirrel," he said. The squirrel brushed his tail on Pete making the old chugger laugh. "Oooh, ho, ho, your tail is tickly," he chuckled before chugging away.

Back at the depot, Koko found out
that her tunnel colour was green.
It was the same as Old Puffer Pete's!

"I hope I don't get stuck behind
Pete," Koko said as she sped away.
It was too big an adventure to go slow!

Koko raced out of the tunnel.

"Woo-hoooo!" she shouted, zipping round the bend. "Go Koko, go Koko, go Koko," she sang.

"Watch out, Mr. Squirrel!" she called, zooming past the squirrels jumping across the tracks.

"Go, Koko!"

Soon Koko found she was stuck behind Old Puffer Pete.

"Let's switch tracks," she said, wanting to zoom off.

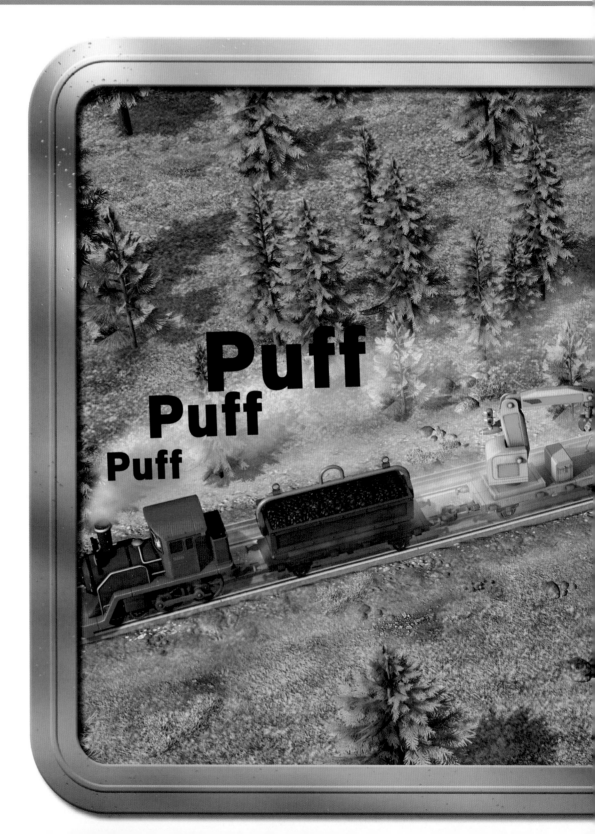

Puff
Puff
Puff

"Oh my, you're going to have an accident carrying on like that. Go slow and steady!" Pete called, but Koko wasn't listening.

Screeech!

When Koko collected her load of timber, she raced to the paper mill.

Suddenly, she saw a baby squirrel on the tracks!

As Koko slammed on her brakes, her load of logs tumbled to the ground.

"Emergency stop!" she shouted, and the squirrels hurried away from the rails. "I'm sorry I was going too fast. I didn't mean to scare you."

Old Puffer Pete had been right; she should have been going slow and steady. How was she going to pick the logs up?

Just then Pete came round the corner, on his way back from the foundry!

"Old Puffer Pete to the rescue!" he said kindly, smiling at Koko.

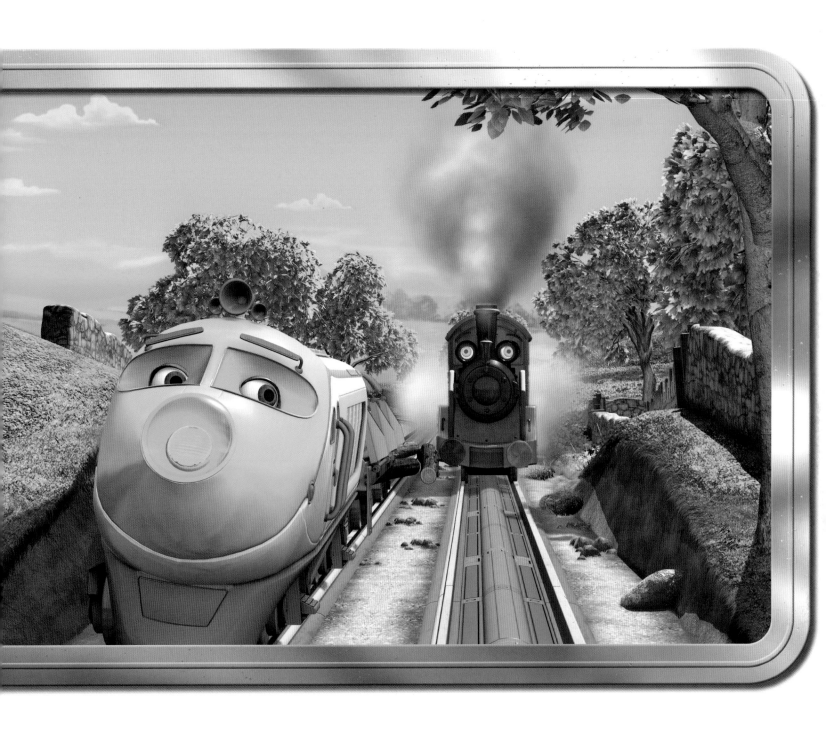

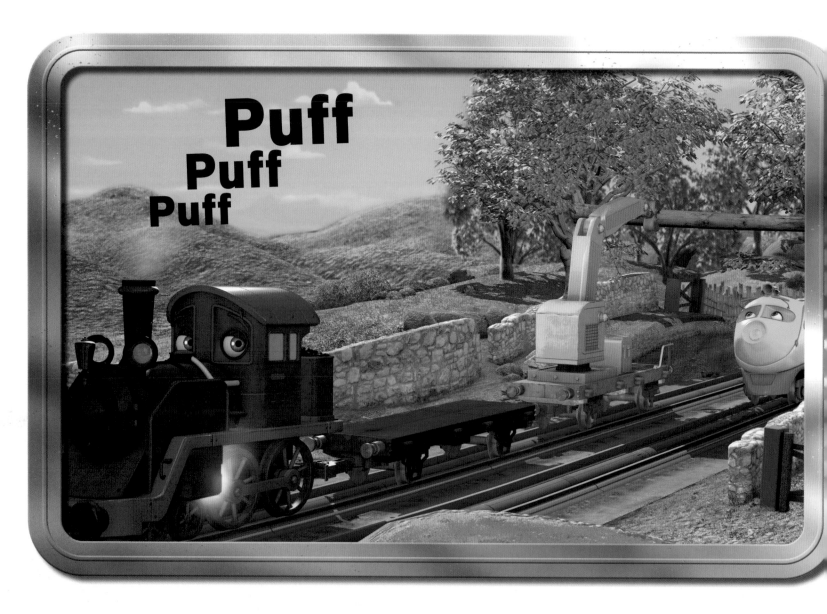

Puff
Puff
Puff

"Thanks, Pete!" Koko said, when he had finished putting all the logs back onto her flatcar.

"I'm worried about the squirrels on the tracks," she said. So Pete used a log to make a bridge between the trees.

"Traintastic! They love it!" Koko said, happy the squirrels were safe.

"Now I've learnt to always take it slow and steady," Koko said as they returned to the depot.

"Whoa-ho-ho. Sometimes it's good to let off some steam," Pete said. "Last one home has square wheels!"

"You're so much fun, Pete," Koko laughed as they raced away.

"Last one home...

has square wheels!"

Zephie's
Zoomaround

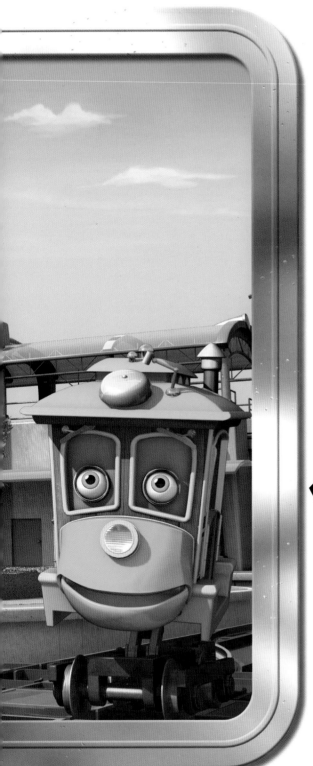

One morning, Brewster and Zephie were going to the farm. A new lamb needed some special food.

"Yipeeeeee!" Zephie yelled, jumping up and spinning round with excitement.

"Yippeee! Yippeee!"

After a while, Brewster started to get annoyed with Zephie, who was talking all the time.

"We're turning now," Brewster said, bored.

"I'm really good at turning!" Zephie said. But when she stopped spinning she found out she was alone!

"Uh-oh…"

Zephie didn't like being alone and started to get worried. She rang her bell, but it was too quiet for anyone to hear. Then Olwin chugged up the track.

"I was looking for the new lamb, but I got lost," Zephie told her, feeling very sorry for herself.

Olwin took Zephie to the repair shed, where Morgan fixed her with a siren. When she turned it on, it flashed and made a loud noise. Morgan told her that the siren was just for emergencies, like if she got lost again.

Outside the repair shed, Zephie found it fun to keep trying out her siren. Brewster and Morgan came to check on her, worried by the loud noise.

"Make sure it's an emergency next time Zephie," Eddie laughed when he realised she was just playing.

Zephie zoomed around Chuggington, searching for an emergency. At the recycling yard, Zephie thought she heard a growling noise. Then she saw some danger signs!

Scared that a lion had escaped from the Safari Park, she quickly set her siren off.

Grrr! Grrr!

Dunbar rushed into the recycling yard to see what the emergency was. Suddenly the growling noise stopped and Irving emerged from behind a wall. The noise had been Irving snoring!

"You mustn't let your imagination ride away with you," Dunbar said.

Zephie carried on looking for an emergency so she could use her siren. At the park, she saw a squirrel in a tree. The squirrel wasn't moving.

"Help! Help!" she called, setting off the siren.

Eddie rushed over and told her that the squirrel lived in the tree. It wasn't stuck at all!

"I don't think you're quite ready for a siren yet Zephie," he said, taking it away.

Zephie felt very sad without her siren and was sorry she had set if off so much. She decided to go and meet the lamb.

The lamb was very happy to see someone new and bleated hello.

"Hello! I mean...baaaaa..." Zephie replied happily. "I can talk lamb!" she giggled.

"Baa!" "Baa!"

Zephie was so excited about the lamb she jumped up and spun around. But then she fell over and couldn't get up! Zephie tried and tried, but she was stuck.

"If only I had my siren!" she yelped.

Felix the farmer found Zephie and quickly telephoned for Calley to come and help.

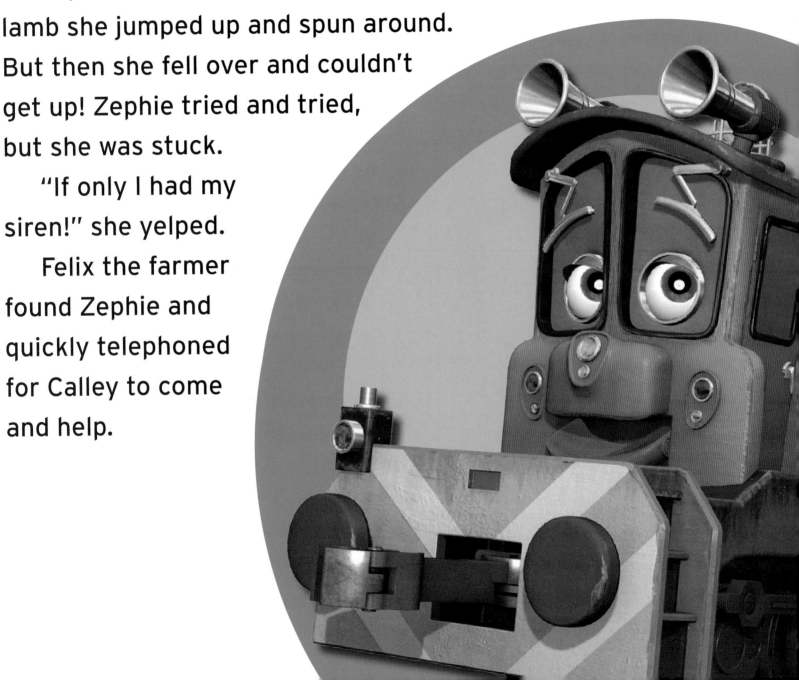

Calley was able to get Zephie ready to ride the rails again, and brought the little chugger back to the repair shed.

Morgan gave her siren back.

"I promise, I'll only use it for real emergencies from now on!" Zephie giggled.

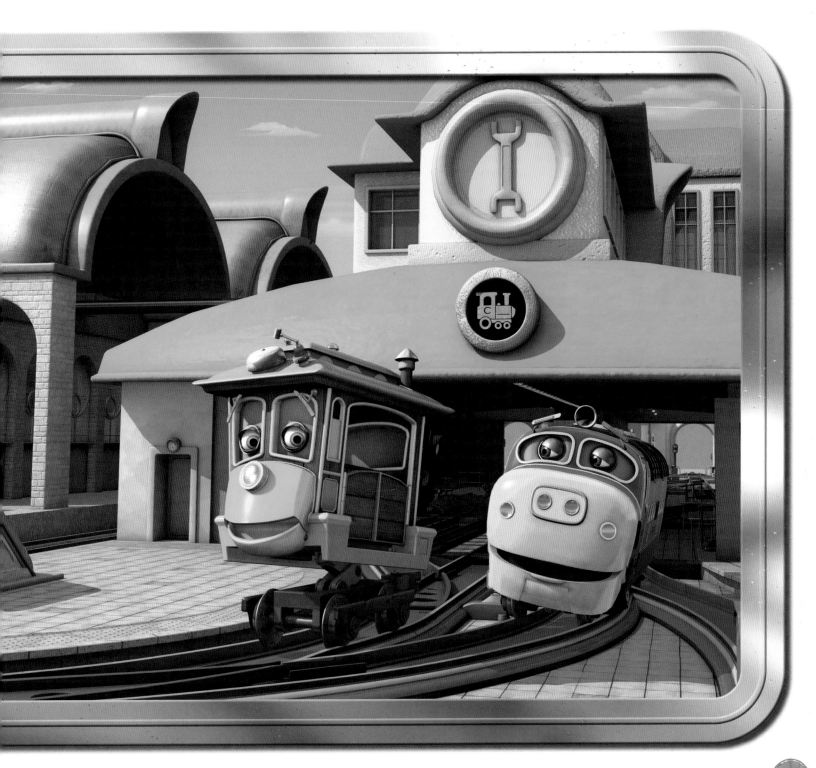

Hodge and
the Magnet

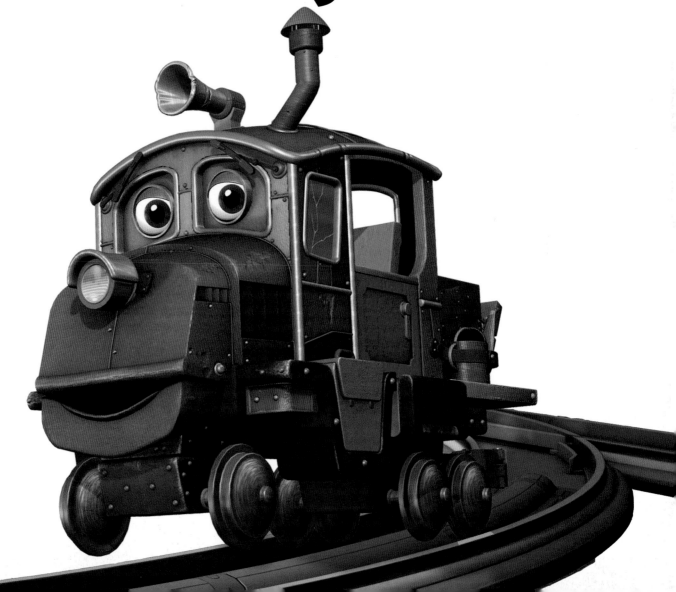

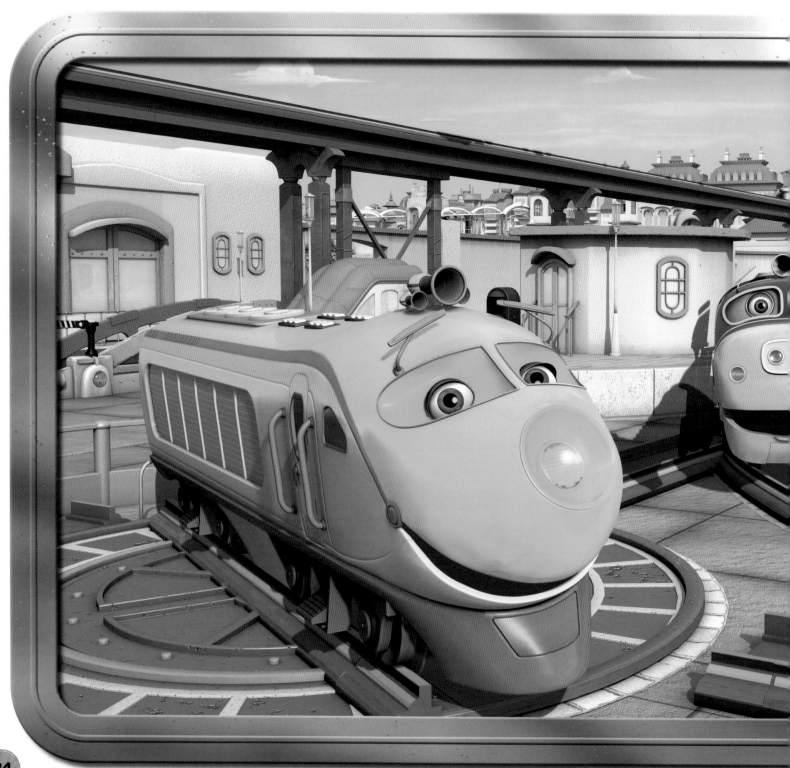

One morning, Chuggington was running very slowly. Part of the yellow line was broken and it was causing no end of problems!

Dunbar told the trainees to make themselves useful around the depot.

"We can do that!" cried Wilson.

Hodge and Calley got ready to mend the track.

"You'll need the magnet to pick up the track," Calley said.

"Just have to get Eddie," replied Hodge, and they set off to collect him.

They couldn't find Eddie anywhere. Hodge went to the repair shed and waited as Emery pulled up, but only Lori got off.

"Oh rivets! He must be running late again," said Hodge.

Just then, Wilson appeared and asked what the problem was. Hodge explained that he was waiting for Eddie, who had to guide the magnet.

"I can help you!" Wilson cried. "C'mon! Let's ride the rails," he said, and they raced away.

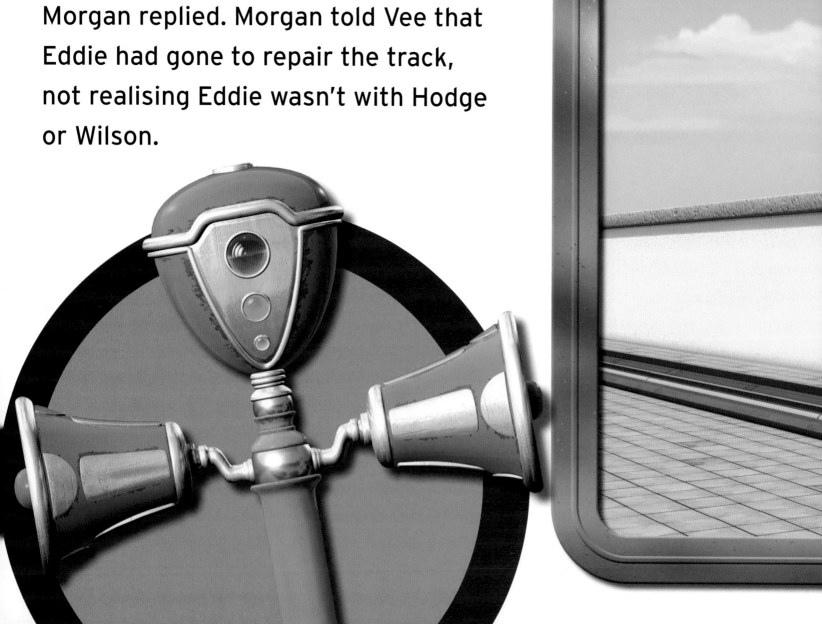

"It's mad today, isn't it Morgan?" said Zephie as they watched the trains leave.

"Poor Vee's got her work cut out," Morgan replied. Morgan told Vee that Eddie had gone to repair the track, not realising Eddie wasn't with Hodge or Wilson.

When Wilson and Hodge found the broken track, Hodge was nervous. He wished Eddie was there!

"I'm relying on you, Wilson, because I can't see," Hodge said as he got into place to pick the track up.

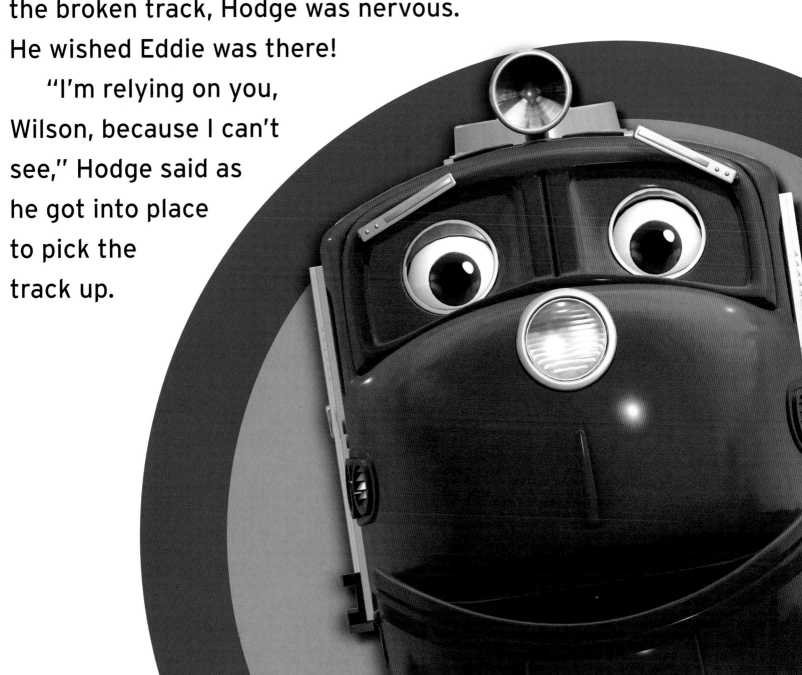

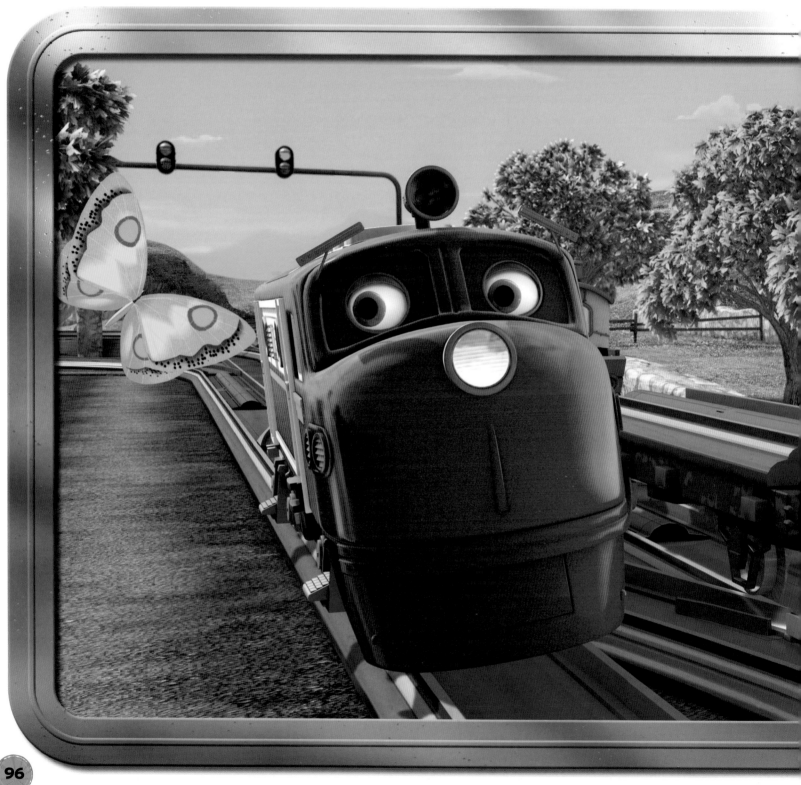

Just then, a butterfly appeared.

"Wilson!" Hodge shouted, worried he wasn't paying attention.

"Sorry! I'm ready," Wilson called.

"Wilson!"

Wilson tried hard to direct Hodge and the magnet. But it was really difficult and the magnet kept missing the rails.

"Up a bit Hodge...down a teensy little bit...back a bit..." Wilson said.

"Aargh! Wilson! You need to be clear," Hodge said.

Wilson moved closer. Suddenly, with a loud
clunk, the magnet leapt onto his face! Hodge tried to yank
it away, but instead he pulled Wilson off the track!

"Oh I never should have let you talk me into this!" he yelped.

After a lot of pulling, Hodge finally managed to get the magnet off Wilson's face by turning it off.

"I can't fix the track. Let's just go back," he said sadly.

"You can do it, Hodge," said Wilson. "Let's try again."

Clunk!

So Hodge swung the crane arm around again. It was going well until the magnet caught the wrong track and moved it out of place.

"You just need to turn the magnet off when you don't need it," Wilson said. "I know you can do it."

Moments later, the track was back in place.

"Perfecto!" Wilson cried with excitement.

Eddie appeared just in time to see the chuggers finishing their work.

"Well done, Hodge, you saved the day!" he said.

"Perfecto!"

Puffer Pete's
Big Party

One morning, the chuggers gathered around Vee to hear some important news.

"Tomorrow is the anniversary of Old Puffer Pete's first day in Chuggington, 150 years ago!" she said.

"The mayor would like us to put on a big show to celebrate, but first we have to distract Pete so it will be a surprise."

Vee asked Pete to go on several jobs so he would be away all day.

"Rattling rivets!" Pete said. "Can anyone come to help?"

"Can't stop!" Brewster puffed by.

"In a rush!" Koko called.

"I'm...busier than a...busy bee," Wilson panted past.

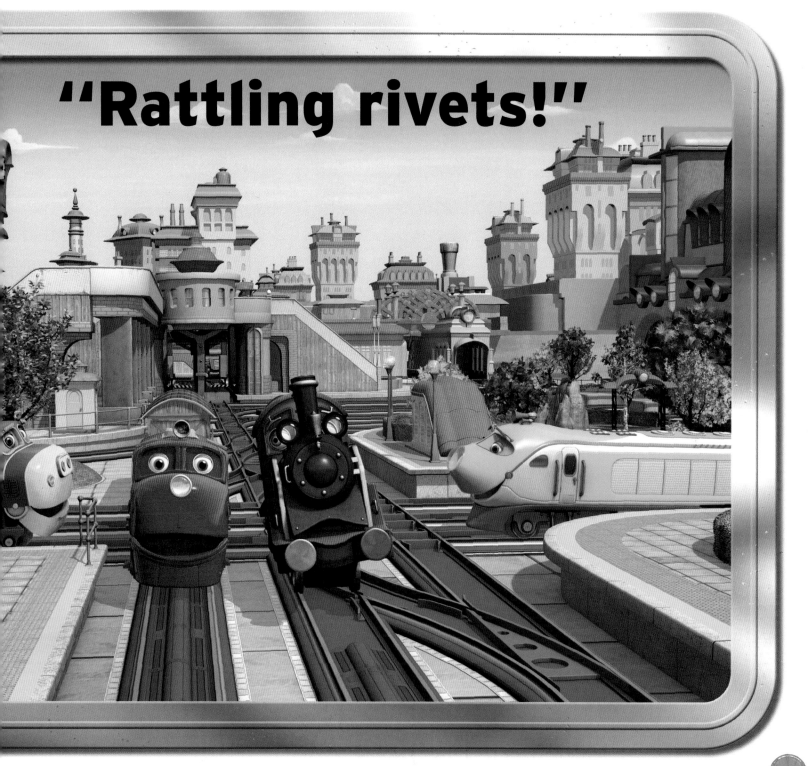

"Rattling rivets!"

"TRAINTASTIC!"

As soon as Pete puffed away through the tunnel, Dunbar told Wilson, Koko and Brewster that they were to be the stars of Pete's big show.

"Traintastic," shouted Koko.

"We're going to be stars!" gasped Wilson.

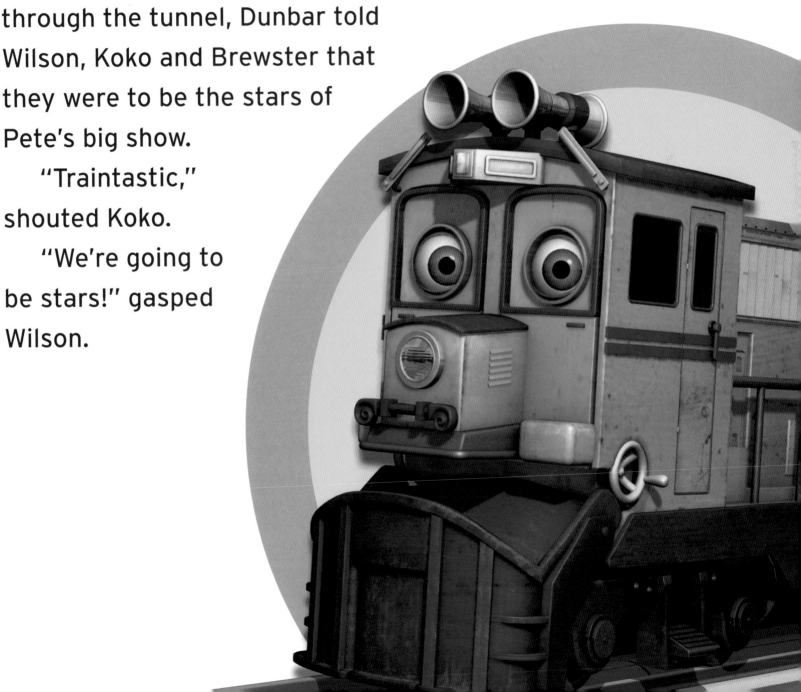

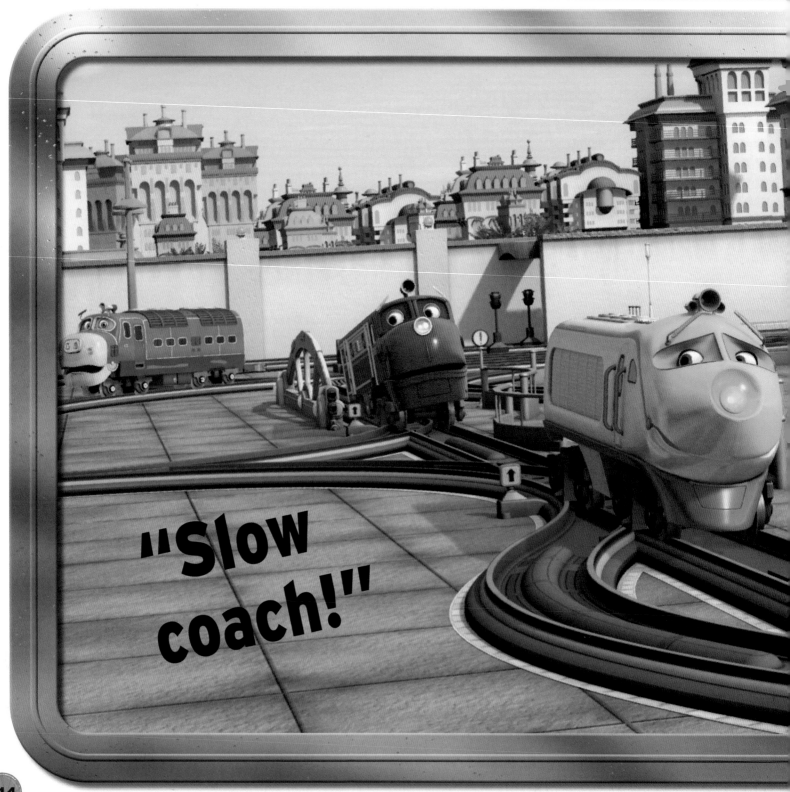

At the training yard, the trainees practised their moves for the show. It was hard work keeping their wheels together.

"Koko, you're going too fast!" grumbled Wilson.

"Am not! You're a slow coach!" Koko shouted back, as Brewster took the wrong track.

Suddenly, Brewster and Wilson crashed
into each other with a loud clunk!
"Honking horns! Look where
you're going will you?" Brewster
said, crossly.
"You should watch out!"
Wilson snapped back.
Dunbar sighed. He didn't
think his engine could
take much more
of this.

Screech...Clunk!

"Oh bumpers!" Wilson said as he made another mistake.

"We might have to cancel the show," Dunbar told Olwin, who was watching them practise.

"Oh no!" Koko cried, "We can't let everyone down!"

"Oh no!"

So the trainees sneaked out in the middle of the night to practise their moves.

"We need to roll together," Koko said. "Let's count out loud: **1**-2-3-4, **2**-2-3-4..."

"...**3**-2-3-4, **4**-2-3-4..." Brewster and Wilson joined in.

"We're doing it! Go, trainees, go!" Koko said excitedly.

"One, two, three, four!"

In the morning, Vee called Pete to the training yard.
"Surprise!" the waiting chuggers shouted.

"Surprise!"

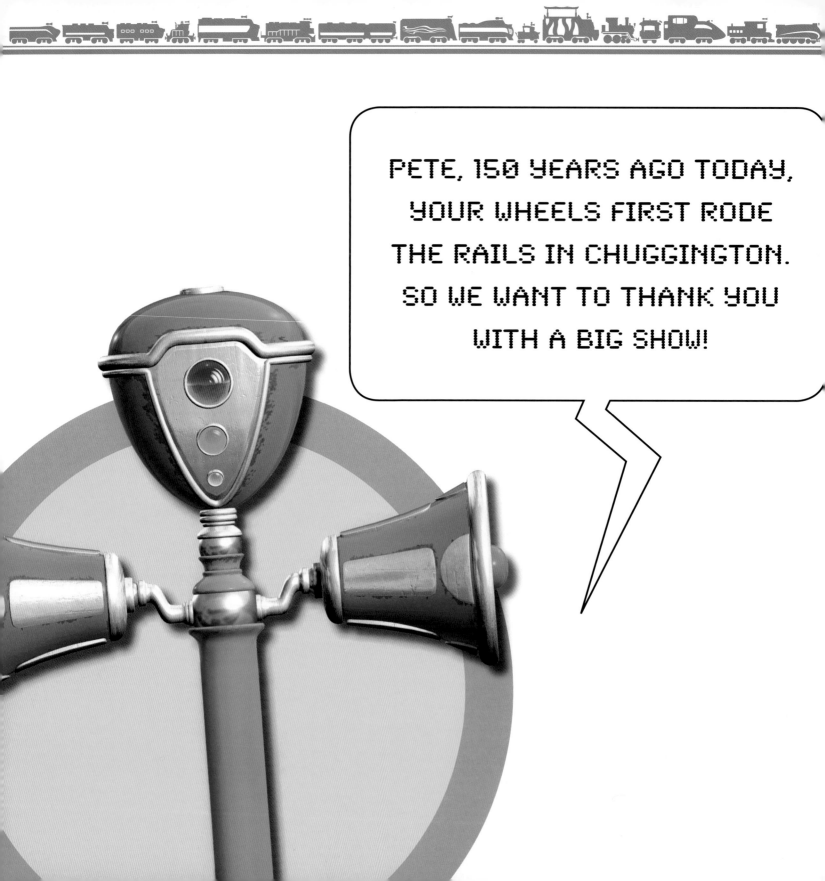

"Rattling rivets!" Pete said happily, as Wilson, Koko and Brewster rolled into place.

125

"The kindest chugger you could ever meet, is our great friend, Old Puffer Pete!

We're trainees and he teaches us a lot. Huffing and puffing, giving everything he's got!" They sang, gliding in time to the music.

"No matter what we do, he never blows a gasket. We're here to tell you, Puffer Pete is traintastic!

So chuggers please, join us as we say, Old Puffer Pete, Happy anniverssssssssssary!"

They cheered, as a flatbed car rolled into view, carrying a surprise for Pete.

Whizz! BANG!

A curtain dropped and a model of Pete was revealed.

"Smashing!" Pete cried. Fireworks whizzed and burst overhead.

"Well done chuggers!" Dunbar said. Everyone cheered!

"Only another 50 years and we can celebrate my 200th anniversary!" Pete said, smiling.

"Oh bumpers! We better start practising!" Wilson laughed.

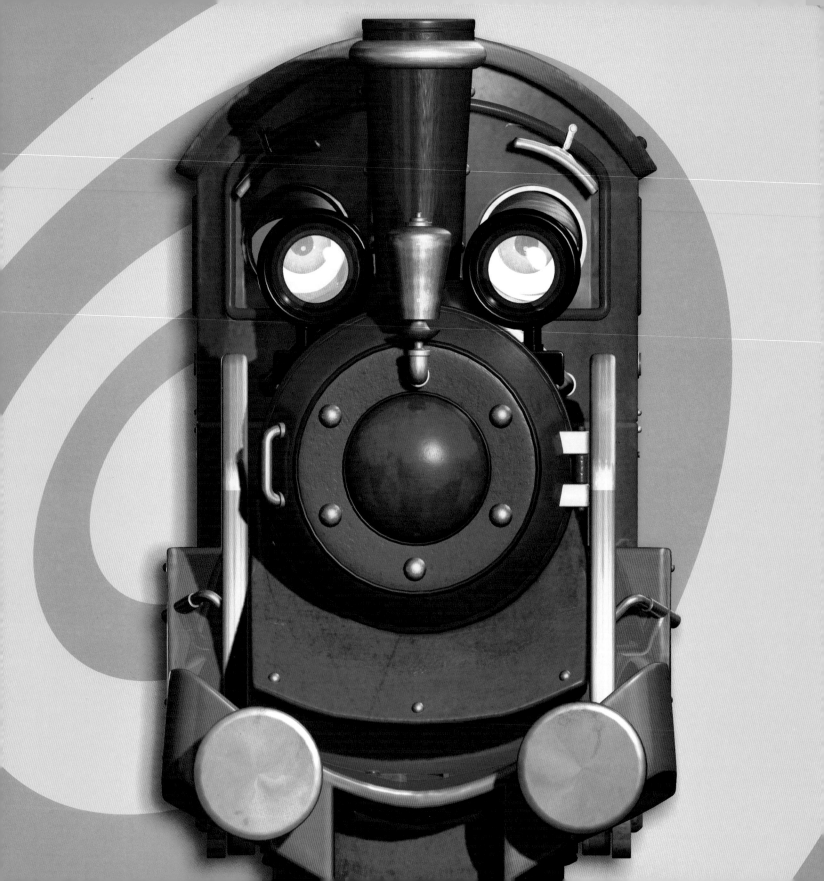

Jetpack Wilson

It was an exciting morning for Koko, Wilson and Brewster. Today they were going to train with Action Chugger, Chuggington's super-hero chugger!

"Ready for action?" he said, landing in the training yard.

"Wheels to the rails!" Wilson said excitedly. He couldn't wait to learn how to fly!

"A super chugger has to stay in shape," Action Chugger said as the trainees pushed and pulled cars up and down a big hill.

"When do we get our flying lesson?" asked Wilson, wanting to have more fun.

"You've got a lot to learn first," Action Chugger said, laughing.

"Now let's see if you can handle an emergency," Action Chugger called from the air.

"Yay!" cried Brewster and Koko.

"Perfecto!" said Wilson. "Real super chugger work! Do we get to use jetpacks?"

"There's more to a super chugger's work than flying, Wilson," Action Chugger replied, spinning in the air.

"Perfecto!"

"Here we are, Heroes," Action Chugger said, pulling up at a tree.

"What? I'm rescuing a teddy?" Wilson asked, rolling his eyes.

"Let's pretend it's a cat. Have no fear, Action Chugger is here," Action Chugger instructed as he guided the teddy safely down to the ground.

"I'm rescuing a teddy?"

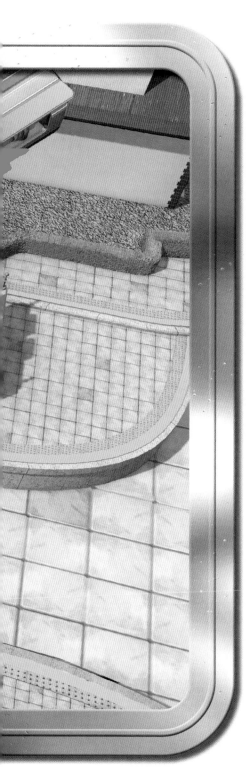

"Don't worry pretend cat...teddy... thingy," Wilson chuckled cheekily when it was his turn to rescue the teddy. "C'mon. I'm a very busy super chugger."

But Wilson wasn't gentle enough and the teddy fell to the ground! "Oh bumpers!" he sighed. Being a super chugger was harder than it looked.

"Oh bumpers!"

143

Later on, Action Chugger took the trainees for a practise
ride on a flight simulator.

"Honking horns, this is fun!" Brewster shouted as he
bounced around in the air. "Look at me, I'm flying!"

"It's only pretend, just like the cat was," Wilson sighed,
feeling grumpy.

Jetpack Wilson

Suddenly, Action Chugger's emergency light started to flash. Someone needed super-hero help!

"Can't I keep practising?" asked Brewster, disappointed that the lesson was over.

"Sorry, it's too dangerous. Maybe tomorrow," Action Chugger called as he flew to the rescue with his light flashing.

FLASH! FLASH! FLASH! FLASH!

Jetpack Wilson

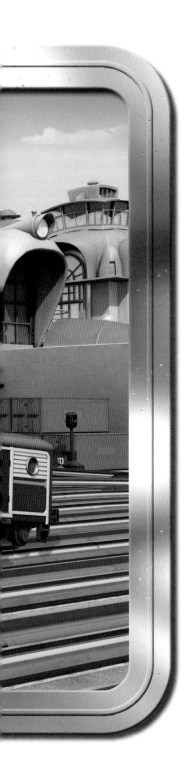

"You know, there are real jetpacks in the loading yard." Wilson said. "Come on Brewster!"

The jetpacks looked so cool, Wilson wanted to try one on. When he rolled under the pack it clamped onto his back with a loud clunk!

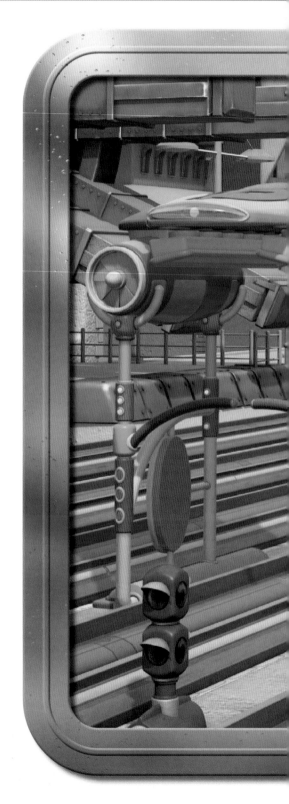

"You better take it off!" Brewster said, worriedly. But Wilson wasn't listening, he wanted to fly!

"I won't go far. Nobody would know..." he said, firing up the jets before Brewster could stop him.

"FIVE, FOUR, THREE, TWO, ONE... ...BLAST OFF!"

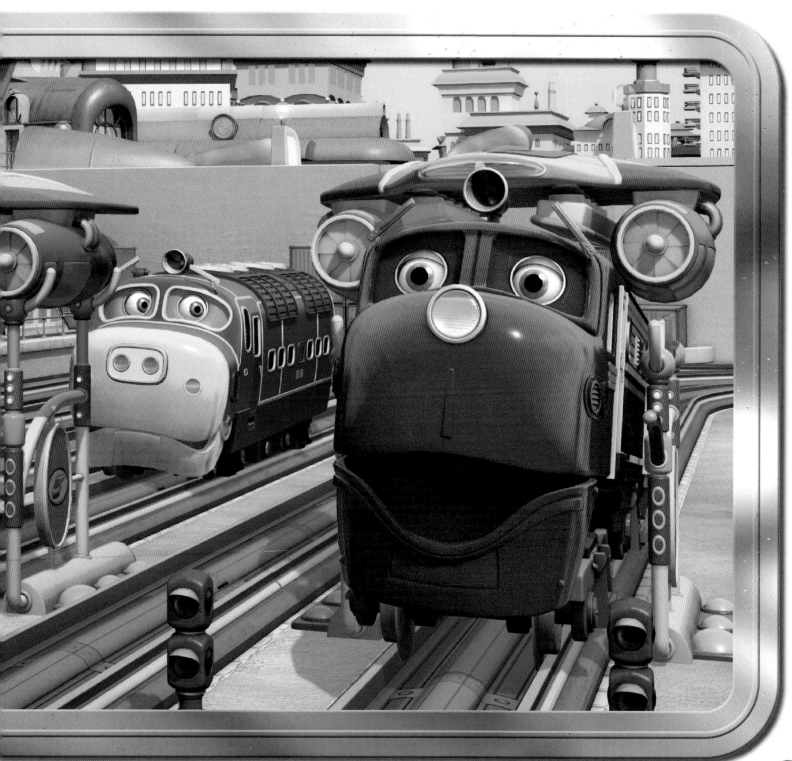

With a loud whoosh, Wilson
took off into the air.

"Woo-hoo! Wahay! Jetpack
Wilson rides the skies," he called,
going higher and higher. Then he
realised he couldn't stop!

"Wilson! Come back!"

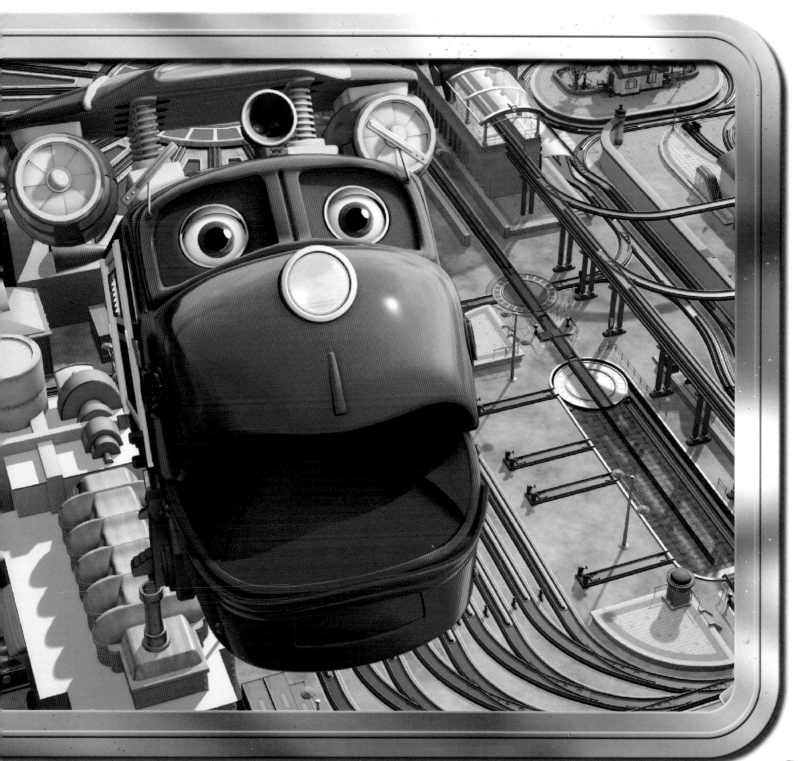

Suddenly, Action Chugger appeared.

"Have no fear, Action Chugger is here!" he said.

He connected his coupler with Wilson and took control.

"Phew! Thanks!" said Wilson, relieved to be safe.

"Hold tight, Wilson, I'm bringing you in."

"I'm really sorry," Wilson said as they landed. "I just wanted to fly like you, but I found out there is more to being Action Chugger than flying, thanks for rescuing me!"

"Wilson, if you learn your lessons and work hard you will be a super chugger. All in a day's work for Action Chugger!" he said, smiling as he took off for another mission.

Traintastic!

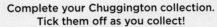

Complete your Chuggington collection.
Tick them off as you collect!

More chuggtastic books to collect!

Stories

- CLUNKY WILSON — ISBN 978-1-4075-6041-0
- CAN'T CATCH KOKO — ISBN 978-1-4075-6042-7
- BRAKING BREWSTER — ISBN 978-1-4075-8009-8
- WAKE UP WILSON! — ISBN 978-1-4075-8010-4
- KOKO AND THE TUNNEL — ISBN 978-1-4075-9530-6
- BREWSTER GOES BANANAS — ISBN 978-1-4075-9531-3

Mini stories

- Braking Brewster — ISBN 978-1-4075-9331-9
- Clunky Wilson — ISBN 978-1-4075-9332-6
- Hodge and the Magnet — ISBN 978-1-4075-9333-3
- Koko and the Squirrels — ISBN 978-1-4075-9334-0
- Wilson Gets a Wash — ISBN 978-1-4075-9335-7
- Zephie's Zoomaround — ISBN 978-1-4075-9336-4

Activity books

- COPY COLOUR POSTER BOOK — ISBN 978-1-4075-6126-4
- STICKER SCENE STORY — ISBN 978-1-4075-6044-1
- Bumper Sticker Book — ISBN 978-1-4075-8141-5
- POSTER BOOK — ISBN 978-1-4075-9529-0
- ACTIVITY BOOK — ISBN 978-1-4075-9422-4

Little library

- MY FIRST LITTLE LIBRARY — ISBN 978-1-4075-6043-4

Multi-play books

- Construct and Play! — ISBN 978-1-4075-9882-6
- MEET THE CHUGGERS — ISBN 978-1-4075-9884-0

Annual

- CHUGGINGTON ANNUAL 2011 — ISBN 978-1-84535-437-4

Activity pack

- CHUGGER TRAVEL PACK — ISBN 978-1-4075-9885-7

3D books

- 3D — ISBN 978-1-4075-8349-5
- Chugger Sticker Colouring Pad — ISBN 978-1-4075-9780-5

Play books

- SING AND LEARN — ISBN 978-1-4075-6127-1
- KOKO ON CALL — ISBN 978-1-4075-8142-2

Story collection

- Storybook Collection — ISBN 978-1-4075-6046-5

Train books

- WILSON — ISBN 978-1-4075-8138-5
- KOKO — ISBN 978-1-4075-8139-2
- BREWSTER — ISBN 978-1-4075-8140-8

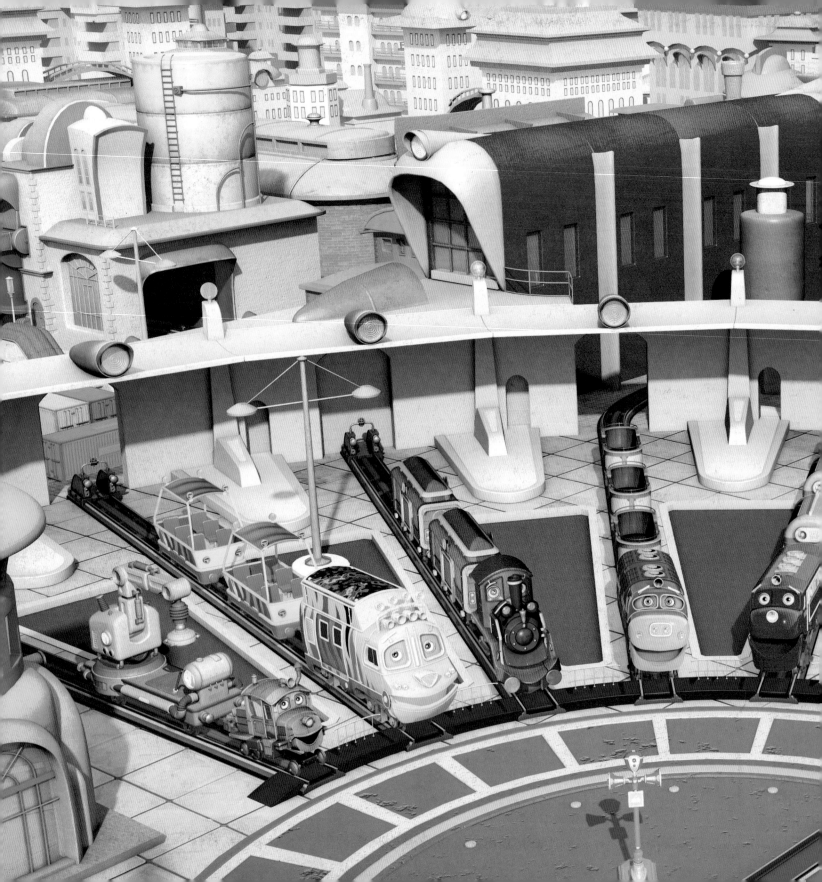